Very Ferry

A Grigsby Series Novella

Robert Maisano

Biplane Media - San Francisco, California

www.robertmaisano.com

Copyright © 2017 by Robert Maisano

First Edition

ISBN-13: 978-0-9994195-2-6

10 9 8 7 6 5 4 3 2 1

Printed in the United States

To you, the early reader, thank you for sharing my work.

Introduction

The idea behind the character of Grigsby Ives Pemberton and his subsequent adventures is an amalgam of experiences from growing up on Long Island's Gold Coast. The place where F. Scott Fitzgerald wrote The *Great Gatsby*. It's the part of New York where tycoons celebrate their wealth, love of family, competition, and opulence.

When I was a kid, I'd read about Vanderbilt, Morgan, and Rockefeller. I envied their success but wondered if they ever laughed. Black and white photos of these Titans showed the same thing: stoic men with silly facial hair, holding the expression like a rod was stuck somewhere it shouldn't be. This confused me. Even at 5 years old I thought, "Do they ever have fun? They have everything they could want!" Perhaps the lack of antibiotics and air conditioning kept them crotchety.

This notion stayed with me as I grew. I've worked in the offices of the U.S. Capitol and for Fortune 500 Financial Institutions. When my other young colleagues spoke of the higher-ups with fear or wonder, I'd imagine them doing things completely differently. I'd ask my colleagues if they thought the boss would ever spend her money on having a miniature pig race, but the pigs all would have to wear top hats. The questions would be answered by a collection of misshapen faces.

I don't understand the people who cannot see the humor in the day-to-day. I guess we better leave them working on the bean counting and TPS reports. For the rest of us who would like to smile at points during the workweek, I've created Grigsby. A satirical series of an extremely wealthy man, with the appetite of a neurotic adolescent, who gets himself into strange situations. I've made the chapters very short, so they can fit into Instagram posts and on other platforms. The chapters can be read in quick hits, 1 to 3 minutes. Ideal for when you're hiding from your boss in the bathroom stall or waiting for that Uber that seems to be perpetually just a block away.

I'll work hard on providing the absolute best stories and ensure Grigsby never holds back.

Talk soon,

Robert Maisano
San Francisco, California

P.S. I've included a short story in the back of the book about Grigsby's time as an intern on Wall Street. It hasn't been published anywhere else except here. I hope you enjoy it.

"Never compete with someone who has nothing to lose."
—Baltasar Gracián

"Whoop, there it is, do it again
The world is fiction
Special effects
You can't believe what's coming next
Sparks of light
Balls of fire
Whoop, what are we living for?"
— Talking Heads

CHAPTER ONE

Clowns on Fire

The fire spread faster than anyone anticipated. The relay race seemed to be going smoothly. Footage later proved a clown tripped over a piece of equipment setting the stage ablaze. It wasn't a good start to the first day of filming *Very Ferry*, Grigsby's new game show.

The FDNY wasn't happy when they arrived. Grigsby shooed them away and motored the ferry further up the Hudson River. The camera crew held onto their equipment and the contestants, three of which were actual clowns, went below to keep warm. The contestants were in prime physical shape, except the clowns. Their regalia didn't help them either, loose-fitting clothing doesn't bode well in fiery obstacle courses.

Ira, Grigsby's attorney and closest friend, came topside to speak to Grigsby. "Grigs, the clown that set the fire has been kicked off the show."

"Good, he wasn't cheery enough anyway. What kind of clown does he think he is?" Grigsby said chomping on a cigar.

"Beside the fire, I think we're doing well. We're just working out the kinks." Ira said. He'd been a good sport about this new venture. Grigsby had made a deal with a group of Tokyo businessmen to bring a Japanese game show to the United States. "Ryuki has been a great translator."

"He better be, it's his native tongue. Hang on," Grigsby sounded the fog horn twice at some nearby paddle-boarders. They scurried by, and the ferry wake knocked them into the water. They screamed profanities, but no one could hear.

"Didn't Mr. Hayakawa say he'd be sending over a hype-man today? He's not on the ferry." Ira asked.

"He'll be here, just a matter of time. Ryuki's happy he doesn't have to host." Grigsby said.

Grigsby anchored the ferry upriver from the George Washington Bridge. He positioned the ship in a way that if any debris or clowns fell overboard, they'd wash up in New Jersey. As he readied the helm, he noticed an orange blur coming toward him.

An orange cigarette boat barreled along like a missile over the surf. Grigsby realized who it was and groaned. Ira asked what was wrong. "Mr. Hayakawa said he'd provide a level-headed hype-man." Grigsby began powering down the engines. He pointed at the huge cigarette boat approaching, "That's Joji, our new hype-man, the least subtle person on the planet."

CHAPTER TWO

Meet Joji

Joji's cigarette boat slowed and approached the ferry. He dressed like a tasteless interior designer from Boca. His wide lapel suit matched the color of his ship's hull, a terrible burnt orange. Joji's sweat made his spray tan glisten in the sun. He climbed aboard and headed to the bridge to meet Grigsby.

Ira nudged Grigsby when he saw their new hype-man approach. Joji held out his arms like a welcoming drug kingpin.

"Grigsby my dear!" He sang out, "Haven't seen you since that karaoke duet in Tokyo."

"Joji, glad you're here but listen, I have to," Grigsby paused, "Manage expectations. You cannot be a lunatic, this isn't *your* show it's *my* show. You're here to hype up *Very Ferry*, not Joji."

Joji tried hiding his displeasure with a faint smile, "Of course Grigsby, I wouldn't dream of it, let's get started where's hair and makeup."

"Pump the brakes fella, anymore foundation you'd look like one of those clowns. Review this," Grigsby tossed him a booklet, "It's the list of obstacles and dangers that may happen."

Joji looked down below and noticed a team scrapping the charred remains of a mechanical bull and a clown wig into the water. He swallowed his fear and complied with the Connecticut billionaire. Joji asked about the fire, but Grigsby only shrugged.

"Get ready Joji, we're filming in an hour, I need you to give it all you got. The contestants are a little shaken after the mishap with the kerosene and that fucking clown. Anyway, the next obstacle will be fun. It's going to involve a couple of nine irons and that beehive." Grigsby pointed at a massive gray hornet's nest hanging off of a crane from the ferry.

"What's the plot of the show?" Joji asked.

Grigsby pretended not to hear the hype-man. He found that the less sense the game show makes and the more danger there is, the higher the ratings can be. "If people will watch the Kardashians tweeze their eyebrows and eat Pringles for hours then this show will be a hit. Your only concern should be hyping this up. Go!"

Joji complied and prepared for the first filming of the game show. He had no idea what terror waited for him.

CHAPTER THREE

Golfing at Bees

Filming began at 3 pm. The contestants walked onto the stage holding golf clubs. Grigsby and Ira watched from above inside the bridge of the ship. The theme song began to play, it consisted of 80's digital synthesizer music mixed with explosions and fog horns. Joji ran onto the stage that was adorned with Japanese writings and energy drink sponsors. He cartwheeled toward the microphone and began his shtick.

"Welcome to *Very Ferry*, the only game show where the body, mind, and spirit is pushed to its absolute limit. We're filming from the Hudson River today, and our contestants are facing a dire challenge."

Ominous digital synth music lured as Joji lowered his voice, "Contestants will be golfing at that hornet's nest. There's only one beekeeper's suit and the first person to strike the beehive will be allowed to get it. The rest of the contestants must fend for themselves!"

The cameras zoomed in on the contestants who were taking practice swings. They tried to smile but couldn't settle their nerves, the hornet's nest was the size of an obese corgi.

Ira leaned over to Grigsby, "Did we test everyone for bee allergies?"

Grigsby's eyes widened, "I guess we'll find out."

Joji counted down and ran for cover at the start. The contestants began lobbing chip shots at the nest. White golf balls sailed through the air and into the river. The clowns seemed the most nervous. Bees must hate clowns too.

"C'mon, c'mon," Grigsby muttered biting into his cigar.

One woman hadn't swung for a full minute, she composed herself and had an elegant swing. The Titleist Pro-V1 arched high and sank right into the nest but didn't fall out. First, there was nothing. Then the sound of a thousand desk fans hummed, and a black swarm emerged. The woman screamed and pulled on the beekeeper suit while all the other contestants dropped their clubs and scattered.

No one was safe. The clowns leaped overboard. Grigsby and Ira were holding each other laughing uncontrollably. The bee attack lasted for ten full minutes. Joji cheered them on until the bees either died or flew away.

What everyone failed to notice were the blue police lights coming in their direction.

CHAPTER FOUR

Anti-Energy Drinks

The NYPD boat pulled alongside Grigsby's ferry. They told the crew to stop filming from the PA system upon their approach, some officers had rifles in hand. Grigsby told Ira he wished they were aboard during the Somalian pirate raid a few months ago.

Two officers climbed aboard and pushed away a fledgling production assistant who held a clipboard. The officers looked more like soldiers than the typical pudgy city cop. They were broad-shouldered athletes holding rifles. The officers wondered why some people were running around the deck and others laughing hysterical.

"Eh! Settle down you bunch of morons." The cop called out, "Who's in charge here?"

Joji came running toward the cops and introduced himself as the lead man. The cops both laughed and asked if his boss was aboard. Disgruntled and embarrassed, Joji lead the policemen to the bridge. The cops opened the door without knocking. Grigsby and Ira were watching reruns of the game show.

"Uh oh," Grigsby said, "Serpico's here."

The statement didn't start things out on the right foot. Ira cooled the police officers down. "Can we get you something to drink?" Ira asked as he opened up the cooler. "We have..." Ira sifted through the ice and only found the Japanese energy drinks. "Soda from Japan."

The two officers looked at each other and shrugged, "Sure." One said. Ira handed them the cold pink cans. Joji thought to warn them but still felt dejected, so he stayed silent.

One officer looked at the small English writing, "*Very Ferry Mango Merry?*"

Grigsby shrugged. After a few sips, the officers spoke to Grigsby and Ira. They said they could no longer film in the vicinity of the City of New York. A production assistant live-streamed today's filming. The police said the fire and bees are too dangerous.

"You're going to have to go upriver or out into the Long Island Sound." The taller officer said, still drinking the energy drink. It smelled of boiled gummy bears.

Ira then spotted a metamorphosis happening, the officer's skin was turning blotchy red and green, like swelling candy apples. The officers didn't seem to notice. Grigsby saw the reaction too. "Are they umpa lumpas?" Grigsby whispered.

Then the officers collapsed.

CHAPTER FIVE

Salty Actors

Grigsby and Ira looked down at the two unconscious NYPD officers. Their skin was hot pink like the Japanese energy drink cans they drank.

"Are they glowing?" Ira asked.

Grigsby nodded and picked up the can to examine it. "Joji, what does all this Japanese writing say?"

Joji squinted at the character and mumbled. "Can cause seizures and sedation."

Ira looked down at the ferry floor where contestants were looking for their hype-man. He told Joji to get down there and ensure no one comes up to the bridge. Ira paced around the room trying to think about what to do with the police.

"Okay we can wait for them to wake up naturally and then explain what happened, they should—"

"That'll take all night, we're running out of time to film. Here's what you can do." Grigsby paused and picked up his radio, "Ryuki get to the bridge, stat."

Twenty seconds later the door opened. Ryuki noticed the unconscious police offers and didn't flinch.

"First, have Joji send all the cameramen and contestants in the ship's hold below deck," Grigsby said. Ryuki radioed Joji's earpiece and relayed Grigsby's orders. It took a few minutes to get everyone down below.

"We're clear," Ira said looking out the windows.

Grigsby smirked, "Good, okay boys, let's carry New York's finest on stage."

After some backbreaking work, the three men were able to prop up the police officers into chairs on stage. Grigsby tossed the empty cans at their feet and began opening more energy drinks and dumping the contents into the water. Moments later there were dozens of empty cans surrounding the snoozing officers. They looked like two frat boys during welcome week at Rutgers.

"Ryuki, go into my golf bag and get some smelling salts," Grigsby said.

"Why do you have those?" Ira asked.

Grigsby looked around, "It helps my golf game and keeps me awake during boring meetings, like at your law firm."

Ryuki returned and handed the smelling salts over. Grigsby fired up the lights to the stage. "It's show time!" Grigsby shouted. He walked over to the policemen and began to open the salts. Grigsby didn't expect what happened next.

CHAPTER SIX

Participation Awards

The two policemen woke up at once. The heavier one reached for his pistol, but Grigsby calmed him down. The bright stage lights were blinding them, Grigsby gave the signal to dim them. The *Very Ferry* theme song faded with the lights. Soon the police saw what lain around them, dozens of pink energy drink cans.

The heavyset one stood up and puffed out his cheeks. Cupping his mouth, he ran for the starboard side of the ferry and vomited overboard. Grigsby was happy the man had the decency to do that off of the ferry. The policeman, now pale, lumbered back to his seat. His partner looked at him, then at Grigsby.

"I don't know what happened, but you're all under arrest." he said.

"What? You two volunteered to be in the show. It was a chugging contest, and you both crushed it." Grigsby said, acting aloof. The cops looked at each other. Grigsby continued to tell a surprisingly detailed description of the fictitious events. Ryuki came down from the bridge and handed the police a gold trophy which was a unicorn piloting a flaming ferry. Ryuki pretended not to know English and disappeared.

"You're both winners!" Grigsby declared. Confetti flared in the air, and bikini-clad models in sailor hats came running over to them for a fake photo shoot. Grigsby claims models in sailor hats are the anger antidote for all men. It seemed to work, soon the police were making poses and high-fiving. Ira came over and showed them back to their police boat, and they motored away.

Ira, Grigsby, and Ryuki returned to the bridge. Grigsby brushed his hands through his hair and exhaled loudly. "Jesus what a clusterfuck." His friends nodded. "Let's get the hell out of here. I've charted a course to the Long Island Sound. We'll anchor off of the coast of Fairfield, Connecticut, where medicated housewives and depraved trust fund babies run wild."

The ferry hauled up its anchors and motored by Lady Liberty. She looked warm in the evening light. A cool breeze swept over the deck and brought hints of trash and fuel scents from Staten Island. Soon they made it out to the Sound with the Gotham skyline shimmering aft in the distance. Skyscraper windows were pinpricks like stars across a black sky. The ferry plowed through the surf and into the night.

CHAPTER SEVEN

Fearless

Filming went on for six days without a hitch. Their new filming location off the coast of Connecticut offered suitable privacy. The Coast Guard, however, did stop by after reports of strange goat noises coming from the ship. Ira assured them there are no farm animals aboard. Grigsby felt there was enough sample footage to make the networks happy. His goal is to have the game show on three primetime slots.

After a full day of negotiating from the deck of the ferry, every network agreed to air the show. The key selling point is the live capability Grigsby presented. Although, one network asked if there were limits to viewers requests.

"Limits?" Grigsby asked into the speakerphone.

"Well aren't your contestants fearful of odd or dangerous requests? The internet is a depraved place." the executive answered.

"My contestants are fearless."

"Fair enough...okay Grigsby, we'll give you Tuesday nights at 8 pm."

Grigsby popped champagne with one hand, the cork nearly blinded Ira. "Thanks, Benjamin, looking forward to doing business with you." Grigsby hung up and poured champagne flutes for Ira and himself.

Hurried footsteps sounded, and Grigsby turned to see Ryuki hustling toward him.

"We under attack?" Grigsby chuckled.

"No," Ryuki said trying to catch his breath, "We got a problem," Ryuki sipped more air into his lungs, "It's Joji. It's serious."

CHAPTER EIGHT

Yakuza

Ryuki pushed his hair back and exhaled, "I saw Joji during a wardrobe change. His tattoos are tebori style, the Japanese way, no gun, only wood and metal rods. I saw the designs, one is an Oni Mask, the demon." Ira handed Ryuki some water.

"What does this all mean Ryuki?"

Ryuki finished his water in a single gulp, "Joji is Yakuza."

"The Japanese Mafia?" Ira asked.

"Keep your voice down." Ryuki said, "Yes. They're horrible people."

"Where is he now?" Grigsby asked.

"On the rear deck. They're filming the Dolphin, ping-pong and banana obstacle course."

Grigsby pounded the table, "Dammit, that's my favorite obstacle."

Ryuki walked over toward the small bar Grigsby setup. He opened the humidor and removed a false floor from the bottom. It contained a silver sub-compact revolver.

"Jesus, do you have guns hidden everywhere?" Grigsby asked.

"Take this," Ryuki said, handing Grigsby the gun.

"I'm not John Wilkes Booth,"

"Take it."

Grigsby pocketed the gun and looked at Ira. "I thought you vetted this guy?"

Ira was staring at the small TV screen watching the contestants catch ping pong balls shot out by Dolphins.

"Ira!"

"Sorry, yes we vetted him. Clearly, it's a pseudonym. And the Tokyo investors we're tied up with must also be connected with the Yakuza."

"Terrific, I got a flamboyant Tony Soprano running my game show." Grigsby stood and looked at the TV. The contestants were now inside a plastic tank that was gushing with seawater, and they're trying to stuff bananas in the holes to prevent themselves from drowning. "What a mess."

Ira looked at Ryuki, "What should we do?"

Ryuki considered this in silence for a long time, "We wait. Study him, and when the time's right, we'll strike."

CHAPTER NINE

Premiere Night

Ryuki agreed to keep tabs on Joji but insisted that the show must go on. So, it did. The following week was the premiere night. The networks green-lit the show, and Grigsby was getting everything prepared for the U.S. debut of the *Very Ferry* Game Show. Joji had spent several hours trying on new neon-colored suits. Grigsby watched him from the bridge while smoking a cigar.

"How can a swashbuckling wimp like Joji be a gangster?" Grigsby asked Ira. He was reviewing insurance estimates for covering the show's dangerous obstacles. "Ira?"

"What? Grigs, I don't know, don't piss him off tonight. He cannot know that we're on to him."

Grigsby pouted and ate some chocolate cake that Bunny made the team. The double fudge layers made him smile. It was no Baked Alaska, his favorite, but it still tasted glorious.

"How's the insurance looking? We covered?" Grigsby asked.

"Almost, I think...I think we're going to be okay. If someone dies were screwed. But maimed or burned, we're covered."

"Good. You, sir, get a nice piece of cake!" Grigsby slid a plate across the table which knocked all the papers down.

"Dammit Grigsby!"

"Sorry. I got excited. Forget that stuff, we'll deal with it later. Take your cake and come with me. We need to get ready for the premiere."

Grigsby didn't know that it was going to be a long, and expensive night.

CHAPTER TEN

Black and White

Off the coast of Fairfield, Connecticut lay a spectacle tonight. A massive ferry, ablaze in spotlights, sat anchored and surrounded by spectating ships. News helicopters circled the area, and people ashore watched the big screens on barges light up the night. The country's latest Japanese inspired game show, *Very Ferry*, is premiering.

Grigsby reveled in the spectacle. He wore his favorite double-breasted suit from Saville Row. Bunny, his wife, gave him a new silk handkerchief that was adorned in tiny ferries and dolphins. He smirked at it and looked down at a nervous production assistant who always seemed to be on the verge of a complete panic attack.

"What are the projected viewership numbers?" Grigsby asked.

"Over 10 million, and climbing, sir."

"Grand, if we can surpass 20 million, I'll buy you a house. 50 million I'll buy you a house far away from dollar stores and fast food establishments."

The production assistant hesitated. "Thank, thank, you sir, I'll do my best."

"No, you won't. Doing 'your best,'" Grigsby made air quotes, "Means you're appealing to *your* standards. I want you aiming for *my* standards which I can assure you are more colossal. Doing your best is a crock of shit. Do your job." Grigsby lit a cigar.

The production assistant looked as if he was about to faint, vomit, or both. Grigsby noticed this and leaned over to the production assistant and reached into his suit pocket. "Here," Grigsby said, handing the production assistant something wrapped in cellophane paper. He unfolded it to reveal a giant black and white cookie from Grigsby's favorite deli. "This is the secret to success," Grigsby said and walked away.

Joji sat in a director's chair getting his eighth layer of makeup applied. He wore a teal suit that had pandas smoking cigarettes on it. He looked to be meditating as Grigsby approached. Grigsby noticed the inkling of a tattoo on Joji's wrist, a Yakuza design.

"Grigsby m'boy! How you be? Fun night yes?" Joji said.

"Yes Joji, are you sure you understand the first obstacle? If it goes wrong, we're toast. That human birdcage looks less stable than a journalist from *Cosmopolitan Magazine*."

Joji waved his hand like he was swatting a fly, "It'll be fine Grigsby, you worry too much. *Very Ferry* will be...very merry!"

Grigsby face-palmed himself, hiding his anger. He turned and walked away shouting "Show time in 15 minutes."

CHAPTER ELEVEN
The Banana Wall

The 80's synth music blared from towering speakers aboard the ferry. Joji ran onto the stage as the cameras went live, marking the first live episode of *Very Ferry* game show. He did a front flip and grabbed the microphone, his hair didn't move an inch as it was caked in so much gel it looked like a baby seal after an oil spill.

"Welcome to *Very Ferry* the world's most difficult game show where the body, mind, and spirit are pushed to their absolute limits. Tonight, we're unlocking true human potential as the contestants will face unimaginable feats." Joji continued his speech while Grigsby and Ira watched from the control room. The production assistant avoided Grigsby's gaze as he leaned over to see the viewership count. Fifteen million people had tuned in. He grinned.

"Are the live chats up and running?" Grigsby asked.

"Yes sir, waiting for your command to start accepting them." the production assistant said.

"Granted."

The *Very Ferry* live-streaming chat-room immediately was flooded with preliminary requests. Grigsby and Ira looked at the screen. Ira gasped and immediately started estimated insurance costs.

"Amazing. They're total savages." Grigsby chuckled.

The show started with the contestants climbing a giant rock wall. The holds were painted purple or red, what contestants didn't know was that some of the holds are fruit, from bananas to apples. Joji sounded the buzzer, and the group scrambled the wall at once. One clown fell twenty feet, and the crowd cheered.

The live chats started and were demanding that the other clown fall. Payments began flooding in to make it happen. Once it eclipsed $5,000, Joji was instructed to fire a t-shirt cannon at the clown who was nearly at the summit of the wall. On the fourth shot, a rolled-up t-shirt hit the clown's red hair and sent him falling. Profits tripled before he hit the ground.

"Holy shit Grigs!" Ira shouted, "This is getting out of hand too quickly."

"Nonsense. We're satisfying the American people's bloodlust."

The show continued, the contestants who survived had to decipher a collection of Caesar box ciphers, an old code training exercise the NSA uses. One woman named Tessa was dominating, she was first over the wall and cracked the code in a minute making her the winner of tonight. The fans loved her.

Grigsby patted Ira's shoulder, "We have a world-class hit on our hands."

"I don't know Grigs, the carnage, it's almost too much."

"There's no such thing," Grigsby waved over the production assistant, "What are the ratings saying?"

The production assistant handed a printed report, and Ira couldn't believe what he was seeing. "That's impossible."

CHAPTER TWELVE

Off The Charts

"Number one?" Grigsby asked.

The nervous production assistant forced a smile, "Yes, we're the highest rated show right now on television across the board."

Grigsby grinned at Ira. "See?"

Ira nodded agreeably at his friend, "You're right Grigs. But that was utter chaos. We cannot sustain this, contestants are going to quit before starting. The odds are stacked against them."

"Wrong. There are no odds, it's pure chance, that's why the viewers love it." Grigsby said.

"Yes, but how can we hedge against something terrible Grigs?"

"I have a plan," Grigsby told the production assistant to leave the room, "Any calamities should be directed onto Joji. He'll be our fall guy. That should weaken his resolve."

Ryuki knocked twice and entered the door to the room. He looked haggard, sunken eyes and pale skin. He pulled up a stool and sat. Ira and Grigsby exchanged surprised glances.

"What the hell happened? You look like Charlie Sheen." Grigsby asked.

"Joji happened. I've been watching him for 65 hours straight. I can't find a single thing to use against him or proof that he's in contact with the Yakuza."

The room stayed silent for a while. The ships internal workings bellowed like a low playing organ. Someone was knocking on the door lightly. Grigsby motioned to Ira to open it, he saw the production assistants face peak in.

"Sir it's the network executives, they want to speak with you."

"Are we being sued?" Grigsby asked.

"Um, one moment." The production assistant whispered into the phone, nodded and looked at Grigsby, "No we're not."

"Good, I'll take the call." Grigsby took the phone and walked onto the bow of the ferry. Ira and Ryuki watched as he seemed to be laughing into the phone. Then he began jumping up and down like a child on Christmas morning.

Ira looked at Ryuki who just gave a weak shrug and nodded off into a quiet nap. Moments later Grigsby came in with a grin ear to ear.

"They love the show and want to give us more time slots. Soon we'll dethrone those inept Kardashians."

CHAPTER THIRTEEN

Bobcat Sandbox

"If we're in line to surpass the Kardashians we can pay off the investors in no time," Ira said, excited to hear the news.

Grigsby nodded, "People watch those mooks play scrabble and speak at a 3rd grade reading level. Our show is far more entertaining."

"But we'll have to raise the stakes Grigs, it's the only way to stay on top."

"The live chat-room recommendations will do that for us, we'll scale that up and allow more carnage," Grigsby said as he sorted through a variety of new silk handkerchiefs for tonight's show.

Ira clear his throat, "I mean to raise the stakes in the less dangerous areas, perhaps more difficult cerebral obstacles?"

"Sure, we can do that," Grigsby said, half listening.

Later that afternoon they reviewed the lineup of contestants and obstacles. The new contestants were an all-male gymnastics team from the Philippines. They looked like clones; they all had 2% body fat, lean cut muscles, and sinew veins. None of them were above 5'4. Grigsby liked them. He knew the obstacle he'd unveil tonight for them. He broached the idea to Ira.

"Where are we going to get 25 bobcats? The Bronx Zoo doesn't have a rental policy." Ira said.

"Don't worry about that, I know a guy. What's going to be tricky is the sand. We're going to need a fuckton of sand. Get Joji to fetch some from the shoreline, have the interns help."

An hour later Joji reluctantly took a tender boat ashore with a pack of their unpaid interns. Joji couldn't tell what made him more upset, the fact his manicured hands will be ruined or the interns ceaseless barrage of questions about what are the life hacks to *success*. "Strangling my competitors." Joji thought to himself. Then he smiled and knew it was time to unleash his masterplan.

CHAPTER FOURTEEN

Enlightened

The night was moonless during the second filming of *Very Ferry*. This made the precipitous tower go on forever in the yellow and pink spotlights. Two contestants had panic attacks upon seeing the obstacle. The Bobcat Sandbox became a trending topic amongst the fans who were tuning in for the pre-show. It was a 15-foot deep sand pit with sheer walls, and 25 bobcats lingered about. Grigsby hadn't fed them in days to make them more agitated.

"No, no they're just like big house cats, no need to worry," Ira said into the phone, he was on the phone with their insurance company who was watching the pre-show from their offices. "Light scratches are the most they can do." Ira looked at Grigsby for approval, but he was busy shining a laser pointer into the pit and laughing.

Ira was able to get the insurance lady off the phone feeling content but not happy. He prayed that the people in the chat-room were feeling less bloodthirsty but had hollow hope. Ira watched the contestants warming up, some were doing pushups, others playing trivial pursuit, another trying to learn Swahili. Preparing for *Very Ferry* is the equivalent of training for space shuttle launch while taking the MCATs.

The Filipino Men's Gymnastics team were on the far side of the ferry alone. Grigsby watched them from one of the TV screens. Despite being on the windward side and getting sprayed by seawater, they were meditating. Grigsby watched them for a long time and gasped when he realized what was happening. The outside temperature was around 55°F, with heavy gusts. The gymnasts should be freezing as they sat there stoically soaking wet. Instead, steam lifted from their bodies. Grigsby knew what this was.

Decades ago, Grigsby took a gap year between boarding school and university. He went on a vision quest starting in Ulaanbaatar, Mongolia and bringing him through Kathmandu, Nepal. Here he met a dying Buddhist. Grigsby spent weeks in the Buddhist's cabin in the foothills of the Himalayas. It was here he learned how to reach a heightened state through deep meditation. He learned how to direct energy throughout his body. Grigsby uses it today to offset hangovers or feelings of dismay after heavily feeding on pork shoulder.

The gymnasts were doing this to attain ultimate strength. Grigsby called his bookie who lives full-time in a bowling alley outside Riverdale. Grigsby spoke to him about a large bet he'd like to place.

CHAPTER FIFTEEN
Off The Chain

The show started, and all of the contestants breezed through Ira's cerebral obstacle, it was a step above bar trivia, he felt dejected. Grigsby watched as they moved toward the physical obstacles. Joji riled up the audience and encouraged the people in the live chat-rooms to demand more from them. Grigsby and Ira looked at each other.

"What's Joji doing? We didn't tell him to say that." Ira asked.

Grigsby stayed silent and watched the screen. Strange demands came flooding in with high payments attached.

"$10,000 for pushing other contestants into the pit? I don't know Grigs,"

"Deny that request, it's too early," Grigsby ordered.

The team of gymnasts lined up to the *Bobcat Sandbox* obstacle. A series of checkered floor tiles lay above the sandpit. Some of them were on hinges and would plunge a person into the pit containing fierce bobcats. One gymnast tested the first tile by hanging onto his teammates in a human chain. He leaned his weight against the tile and watched it collapse, they held on to him. The crowd cheered, thirsty for carnage. The team huddled and devised a plan.

Joji came over and yelled at them in Japanese, he didn't like any planning from the contestants. "You go! You go now!"

The team of nervous gymnasts recreated the human chain and began hopping from tile to tile. As some collapsed the others yanked the falling men skyward. It was as if the members of *Cirque du Soleil* were playing a dire game of *the floor is lava*.

Grigsby marveled at the ballet of the team. He muttered something about chaotic beauty but winced when he saw half of the team fall on separate tiles at once. The human chain broke. Screams cried from below along with the roar of cats. The ones above ground remained alone on their tiles. Joji yelled at them to move and ordered the audience to throw pastries at them as encouragement.

"Grigs that wasn't a request from the chat-room, Joji has gone rogue," Ira warned.

Moments later another gymnast fell through a trapped door tile into the pit, the remain two ran for the end of the obstacle, and both perished.

CHAPTER SIXTEEN

Laddering Up

Cries and feline wails bellowed from the sandpit. The entire gymnastics team was doing their best to fight off the bobcats. The cameras inside the pit captured the carnage in low light. Ira and Grigsby watched nervously from the TV monitors.

"We should send in the safety teams," Ira advised.

"No, let's see what the chat-rooms say," Grigsby leaned over the production assistant, "Sitrep."

The production assistant spoke low, shocked by the requests he was seeing, Grigsby, nudged him urging him to speak up. "Sir, they're saying we should leave them in the pit. We're almost at $100,000 in payments too."

"Incredible," Grigsby said. "And I saw the demographics earlier today. Most of the viewers are middle-aged housewives. Who knew they held such a vicious bloodlust?"

"Grigs, we can't leave them. We—" Ira couldn't tell what he was seeing on screen.

The gymnasts were throwing the cats off of their brethren. Then they began to pile on each other against the sandpit walls. Soon four men stood on each other's shoulders, the other teammates climbed up the human ladder. Soon they reached the lip of the sandpit. The crowd screamed a collective "ahhh!" as they saw the last man climb up the ladder and out of the pit.

The man who made it out, lay on his stomach and clasped onto the forearms of the top of the human ladder. He shouted something in Filipino, and the bottom man on the ladder began to climb up the other men. Soon he made it out of the pit and held onto the ankles of the topside man. The process repeated itself. Bobcats jumped onto the men as they made their escape. Two bobcats climbed all the way out and fled into the audience.

Moments later the entire team of gymnasts stood on the other side of the obstacle, covered in bloody scratch marks and deep lacerations. But they were victorious, and the crowd went wild. Grigsby's bookie texted him a series of cash emojis. It was the wildest spectacle in game show history.

CHAPTER SEVENTEEN

Pemberton Investments on Lex

The aftermath was absolute lunacy. The Filipino gymnastics team became an overnight sensation. The next day they were interviewed on every morning talk show. Grigsby was by their side translating and spreading the word of his new game show. Technically, Ryuki was translating to Grigsby's earpiece, but no one noticed.

After the morning show circuit, Grigsby returned to the *Pemberton Investments* offices in the Chrysler Building. He loved the silver art deco tower but hated its location.

"Midtown, especially Lexington Avenue, is a gutter of filth surrounded by dry cleaners and foul delis, there's no charm here," Grigsby explained to the gymnasts in the limo. They nodded politely.

Back in the office, Grigsby led the team to a separate conference room where they met with Becky Pemberton, Grigsby's daughter. She started a new yoga company and wanted to sponsor them. Grigsby felt confident in his daughter and let her take the reins. Grigsby headed for his office.

Caitlyn, Grigsby's secretary, was walking briskly on her treadmill desk outside his double door office. Grigsby didn't understand fitness, especially fitness at the office. It was too Orwellian for him. It made him feel as if she were a hamster in a pantsuit.

"Any messages from the networks?" Grigsby asked.

Caitlyn sucked water from a long rubber straw, "Nope." She said with a smile.

"Ira in there?" Grigsby asked.

Caitlyn nodded.

Grigsby opened the double doors in a clean motion. A monolith of granite and white marble stood against the floor to ceiling windows. It was his grand desk that stretched to the corner of the office. The views looked north toward Central Park and panned to the East River. Grigsby stared at the great red *Pepsi Cola* sign on Long Island City and felt thirsty. Ira sat by the Aegean Bordeaux Marble fireplace, the hearth warmed the entire office. Brahms played softly through the intercoms in-wall speakers.

Grigsby smiled, pleased with the upward direction of his new venture. He looked at the brass bar cart, checked his watch and shook his head. He opted for a doughnut from the black and white *Sees Candy* cart. Grigsby walked over to Ira and noticed he was asleep with his mouth agape. Grigsby smirked and began tossing chunks of doughnut at his attorney, his mouth being the bullseye.

As he sank one in perfectly, Ira stirred awake coughing. "Dammit, Grigs!" Grigsby chuckled.

Then the intercom buzzed and interrupted Brahm's *Hungarian Dances* with Caitlyn's voice. "Mr. Pemberton, it's urgent, something has happened to Ryuki."

CHAPTER EIGHTEEN

Poisoning the Butler

Pemberton Investments has a full-time medical staff in the east wing of the office. They prep employees who are traveling into the jungles of underdeveloped nations. The medical staff is often treating two common ailments: panic attacks and gout. The latter known as King's Disease is brought on by excess consumption of red meat, scotch, and cake. Today the staff wasn't treating either of these ailments. Instead, it was poison.

Grigsby rushed into the medical room. Ryuki was lying on a table, his skin the color of a fish belly. The lead doctor, Vanessa Myles, stood, snapped off a latex glove and shook Grigsby's hand.

"The blood work came in, and it appears there are trace amounts of cyanide and iridium in Ryuki's system. We're treating this by restoring fluids and giving him 100% oxygen and hydroxocobalamin—" Grigsby gave a confused look, "It's Vitamin B12a." She said.

"He'll pull through this?" Grigsby asked.

Dr. Myles nodded, "We're monitoring him closely, a nurse will be in the room at all times."

"How'd it enter his system?"

"We're still trying to determine the cause, but I'd say it was most likely ingestion."

There was a knock on the door. Ira poked him in, "Grigs the NYPD are here." Grigsby told them he'd be out in a moment.

"Ingestion..." Grigsby thought for a moment and slammed his fist on the table. He thought back to the night after filming *Very Ferry*. Joji offered desserts from Tokyo, they were daifuku and mochi. Grigsby and Ira declined as they were about to head to the country club for steak night. "Ryuki couldn't resist the sweets from his home. Dammit!" Grigsby stormed out of the room.

Outside NYPD officers were talking to Jacques, the head of security for *Pemberton Investments*. He was from Nigeria and about the size of a Volkswagen, he played for Ole Miss as a linebacker then joined the Marines. Jacques ran security operations for employees around the globe. Grigsby walked over and shook the officer's hands.

"The commissioner sent a team of officers to guard the premises and the penthouse on Park Avenue," Jacques said.

They briefed Grigsby on the specifics of the added security. When the officers left, he asked to speak with Jacques alone.

"Do the police know about Ryuki?"

"No sir, per your instructions I omitted that fact."

"Good, we don't want any written record of this. The Yakuza are everywhere."

"Understood, how can I help?"

Grigsby looked up at Jacques, "This is something I have to handle on my own."

CHAPTER NINETEEN

Churros, Convicts, & Lax Bro

Grigsby looked at the screens in the control room aboard the ferry. Tonight, was the third episode of *Very Ferry* game show. On the screen was Joji, the hype-man who poisoned Ryuki. Grigsby controlled his anger and reviewed the plan in his mind. Ira wanted to help, but Grigsby wouldn't allow it.

"I must avenge my friend alone," Grigsby said drinking a chocolate milkshake, he wiped his mouth, "Plus, it's good for my attorney to be ignorant of such a situation."

Ira rubbed the back of his neck nervously, "Whatever you say Grigs," Ira said, "Be careful."

Grigsby finished his milkshake and watched the opening theme of *Very Ferry* start. The viewership had tripled since their last show, and the chat-rooms were at capacity. Joji walked on stage, this time looking like a 1980s weatherman on Telemundo. He waved a manicured hand at the new contestants. There stood the "fresh out" crew from Rikers Island, a collection of convicts who looked like tattooed heaps of muscle and veins.

The next installment was a lacrosse team from a New Hampshire board school. They wore neon pinnies and backward snapbacks. The title of the episode tonight is "Convicts vs. Lax Bros." Grigsby knew this was the time to get even with Joji.

The show started with a churro eating contest. A mariachi band swung from harnesses while playing *El Toro Relajo*. Chubby Mexicans in giant sombreros were red-faced as they belted out the classic song. The Convicts were dominating. Cinnamon and dough flew through the air as the Lax Bros scarfed down the Mexican treats. The crowd cheered for the lacrosse players, which angered the Convicts. The Mariachi band played amongst the chaos.

The next event was dangerous. Safety officials moved the crowd to another part of the ship and issued goggles and earplugs. The name of the obstacle said it all, "Hot Potato Flash-Bang." A flash-bang grenade is used by SWAT teams to incapacitate a room of combatants. It's non-lethal, but the flash and shock of the grenade can bring about unconsciousness. Contestants held goalie sized lacrosse sticks and had to pass a live flash bang grenade to each contestant before tossing it into the water. If they cannot do it in time, it explodes.

Ira couldn't bear to watch it, he knew this would be the final straw. The insurance companies wouldn't back them after this. Grigsby leaned in closer to the monitor, his eyes fixed on Joji. Now was the time strike.

CHAPTER TWENTY

Hook Line and Sinker

Grigsby watched the contestants pick up the flash-bang grenades and lacrosse sticks. Joji instructed them on what to do. The Lax Bros smirked, knowing this was an easy win. The Convicts nervously looked around asking if these were real grenades. The audience was as silent. It felt more like the final putt on the 18th hole of *The Masters* than a psychotic Japanese game show.

Joji stepped back and put on his hearing protection and gold sunglasses. He hit a gong to start the challenge. Both teams pulled the pins and began tossing the flash-bang grenades to each member. The Lax Bros did this with ease. But with each pass, the audience gasped as they watched the live grenade sail through the air. The final lacrosse player chucked the grenade overboard, the sea lit up and bubbled. The Convicts were sweating but doing well until one of them dropped the grenade.

"Hit the deck!" Joji screamed.

The shattering boom blinded the Convicts. Everyone held their ears while rolling on the ground. The audience screamed, laughed, and applauded. The Lax Bros picked themselves up and rubbing their eyes. The Convicts, who were in the center of the blast, remained incapacitated. Joji went to a commercial break and sent in the safety teams.

Grigsby refreshed the chatroom requests and approved a challenge. When the commercial break ended, the production assistant informed Joji of the new request. Joji read it aloud.

"Our latest requests from the chat-rooms are asking..." Joji paused, "For me to join the contestants?"

The audience cheered and started chanting, "Joji! Joji! Joji!"

Joji had fear in his eyes but couldn't dismiss the spotlight. He's addicted to the fame. He walked over and picked up a lacrosse stick and flash-bang grenade. Joji took off his suit jacket and rolled up his sleeves exposing his tattoos of Oni demons, foo dogs, a koi, and a dragon. He pulled a headband from his pocket and wrapped it around his head. Closing his eyes, you could see Joji was taking deep breaths. When he opened them, the fear was gone.

Joji nodded at the cameramen to begin filming. Joji would be playing with the convicts that were conscious. The convict held the flash-bang grenade and pulled the pin. No one foresaw the horror that came next.

CHAPTER TWENTY-ONE

Pyrrhic Victory

The flash-bang grenade sailed through the air toward Joji. The crowd was silent. Grigsby held his breath. Joji's stare locked onto the airborne ordinance and caught it in the lacrosse stick.

The crowd gasped. Joji smiled and looked at the last convict, a massive man with a black eye. Joji must pass it to him, and after that, it can go in the water. Joji leaned back and tossed the grenade toward the battered juggernaut. The grenade sailed by the lacrosse stick and bounced along the deck. Joji's eyes widened as he saw the grenade bounce down the deck and into one of the engine's ventilation stacks.

A terrified silence hovered for what felt like ages.

Grigsby looked at the schematic of the ship and realized where it was falling to. He grabbed the PA system mic, "Everyone—" an explosion rattled the ship and the concussion made audience members fall from their seats. Several more explosions sounded and fire and wood splintered from beneath deck. A series of ruptures burst and popped through the ferry. The grenade had fallen into engine system and ignited the gas lines.

Fire roared out of the engine bay as if the gates of hell had been opened. The ferry began to list. Camera equipment and obstacle props slid across the deck, and the audience and staff screamed. Grigsby and Ira were on the bridge watching the events below unfold.

"Sonofabitch," Grigsby said, pulling on a lifejacket. "This is why we can't have nice things." He kicked open a box of flare guns and threw them at Ira. "Go to the leeward size and shoot those off, I'll radio for help." Grigsby began sending a mayday distress call and reading off the coordinates. The ship listed further to a 55° tilt. Grigsby hit the abandon ship button. The safety crews began inflating orange life rafts.

The Lax Bros panicked and jumped overboard, helping no one. The Convicts stayed and assisted the audience.

The stern of the ferry began to dip into the bleak surf. Grigsby phoned a nearby yacht club for help, "Bring me my *Chris Craft*, I'm not going in another damn lifeboat." he hung up. Ira stood close by and looked at Grigsby.

"Where's Joji?" Ira asked.

"I thought you had eyes on him?"

"I lost him in the chaos."

Grigsby and Ira searched the deck as it was splintering apart and couldn't find their Yakuza hype-man anywhere. He had vanished.

CHAPTER TWENTY-TWO

Aftermath, Something Special

The ferry didn't sink. It submerged to the point where only high structures of the ship peaked above water. Ira kept stressing this point as it will help their case with the insurance companies. The Sound is shallow, and the ferry lay in the rocky mud.

Grigsby was the last to leave the ship. It was an elegant sight. A hand-polished mahogany *Chris Craft* from 1960 pulled alongside the ferry. On the bow, the Pemberton family burgee swayed gallantly like a battle banner. The woman piloting the powerboat was a captain from the nearby Pinemont Yacht Club. Her name was Sofia, and she was the most talented sailor on the Long Island Sound.

Sofia piloted the vintage motorboat alongside the listing ferry. She didn't seem to notice the insanity of the scene before her. The *Very Ferry* game show music theme was still blaring from a submerged speaker and dolphins were swimming about as they were released from their tanks. Sofia tossed a line along a railing post and steadied the ship. She extended a hand to help Ira aboard, he was holding a briefcase of legal documents. Grigsby gave one last look at the ferry, bit into his cigar, and jumped aboard. "That went as well as Snapy's IPO," he said.

"Welcome aboard Mr. Pemberton," Sofia said untying from the ferry. "We have champagne and pretzels in the cooler."

"Thank you, Ira open them both. Sofia hand me that searchlight." Grigsby said. He asked her to circle the wreckage, they needed to find Joji.

The lifeboats clustered by a nearby buoy as the Coast Guard ships came to their aid.

The *Chris Craft* circled the wreckage for a half hour and found nothing. The Coast Guard announced that Joji was the only missing person, everyone was okay.

"You think he drowned?" Ira asked.

"Well, since he poisoned Ryuki, I kind of hoped he did. But I wanted him to lose publicly so his employers could see. Shame is worse than death." Grigsby said, pointing the spotlight around the white spume and dark surf.

The cackling sound of dolphins rang out, Grigsby ignored them. Sofia looked over and saw a sight that she'd remember forever. "Um, Mr. Pemberton, you're going to want to see this."

The spotlight lit up the scene. Several dolphins were pushing an orange and gold heap toward the Chris Craft. It was Joji. He turned over and wailed, he was missing an arm.

CHAPTER TWENTY-THREE

Private Victory, Public Defeat

Grigsby pushed the dolphins away and heaved Joji aboard. He lay across heaps of towels on the stern. Grigsby didn't want to stain the deck. Joji moaned as Ira and Grigsby looked for more injuries, besides the arm, he was okay. Grigsby went to use his Ferragamo belt as a tourniquet but didn't want to sacrifice it. He grabbed a line and used that instead. Joji wailed.

"Shut up," Grigsby said. "This is karma Joji."

"Wha, what?" Joji moaned.

Grigsby leaned in close to Joji's red face, "I know you poisoned Ryuki,"

Joji's eyes squinted, and he began to chuckle, "He's Samurai, it needed to be done."

"Well you failed, Ryuki is alive and well,"

Joji tried to hide his reaction but couldn't. "Look, Grigsby…"

"You're done Joji," Grigsby pulled the line tighter, "Your little mission failed and publicly brought shame to your investors. You sank the ferry."

Joji's fate settled in and his eyes closed as he began muttering in Japanese. Grigsby and Ira left him there and had Sofia motor him to the Coast Guard ship. The servicemen and women helped Joji aboard, and Grigsby checked on everyone. He promised they'd be compensated for the unpleasant evening. Then he asked Sofia to bring them back to Pinemont Yacht Club. He didn't want to deal with the press that would be waiting for him a few harbors down in Greenwich.

The hum of the powerboat lulled Ira to sleep. Grigsby stood beside Sofia and breathed in the salt air. The night was cold, but zephyrs from shore warmed them. He took a long drag on his cigar causing the ember to glow brightly.

"What is life Sofia?" Grigsby asked.

Sofia looked at Grigsby, his eyes looked like sapphires against the night sky. "In life we're falling, falling fast, but the good news is, there's no ground." Grigsby nodded, and they beat on against the tides.

CHAPTER TWENTY-FOUR

Fiscally Fearless

Pinemont Yacht Club is home to overextended Wall Streeters who are stuck in middle management. Range Rover lease payments, private school tuition, and mortgages on their castles keep them in a fiscal quagmire. They're one stock market blow from complete financial ruin and do everything they can to hide the cracking façade.

They're a happy bunch though after a good sail, or if they shot below par that week. Tonight, though the clubhouse held a tense and somber tone. It was bonus season, and it looks like they'd be spending most of their sleepless night thinking about corporate growth opportunities instead of the lift lines at Aspen.

Grigsby entered the clubhouse and scanned the room. He saw men who considered themselves titans of industry but moved past them in search for actual kings. He walked fast through trophy-lined halls and black and white photos of tall ships. Soon Grigsby entered the map room and looked through an old bookcase. Ira caught up with him, Sofia too.

"To the left," Sofia said.

Grigsby nodded and grabbed hold of the *Annapolis Book of Seamanship*. Yanking it outward a latch fell behind the bookshelf, and a door opened to the side of it. The trio entered a narrow corridor that smelled like a dry, dusty attic. Soon they entered a wide room at the top of the clubhouse. It overlooked the bay which was as black as oil. Sofia flicked on the lights. An elegant boardroom with two phones, one black, the other red, sat in the center.

"Setup it up," Grigsby said.

Ira opened the briefcase and took out a strange looking laptop with a satellite uplink. It looked more like a device used for drone strikes in Kandahar Province than something a Jewish lawyer would be lugging around. Grigsby took this time to check on Ryuki. He picked up the phone and dialed the hospital that sits along the East River. The nurses said Ryuki was pulling through at triple the speed. They'd never seen anything like it. Grigsby told the nurse to pass along a message, "The Oni has fallen." Grigsby hung up.

"We're online," Ira said,

Grigsby turned to face the laptop screen. A grey-haired man with a stone jawline stared back. He gave a curt bow and spoke, "Grigsby Ives Pemberton,"

"Mr. Hayakawa, good to see you."

CHAPTER TWENTY-FIVE

Tokyo Dreams

Grigsby stared at Mr. Hayakawa, the financial backer of *Very Ferry*, he did not look happy.

"I trust you've heard the news?" Grigsby asked.

"No, we didn't need to, we saw it happen live, and then the feed cut out. Did the ship sink?"

"Yes. Thanks to your man."

Mr. Hayakawa shook his head annoyed. "He's brought dishonor to his family."

"Yeah and he's no Mr. Rogers either, I know who he's Yakuza."

Mr. Hayakawa's face tensed, but he remained silent, waiting for the other shoe to drop.

"You better find Joji and put him on the next flight to Tokyo,"

"Now you wait—"

"If you don't comply, Mr. Hayakawa, I'll inform Homeland Security that your company is backing a terrorist organization."

A heavy silence lingered, Grigsby waited for his investor's response.

The Japanese man folded his hands. "Very well, Joji will fly home tonight."

Ira smiled and mouthed "Thank God." Grigsby smirked and looked back at the screen, "Back row, middle seat, preferably between two people from one of those square states where their waistbands are elastic."

"What?"

"Never mind. Just get rid of him."

Grigsby continued negotiating with Mr. Hayakawa. After a long discussion with many obscure metaphors and corporate bullshit terminology, they reached a favorable resolution. The investment Grigsby owed Mr. Hayakawa had been cut in half, provided Grigsby never reveals the truth about tonight's snafu to the American press. They both agreed, and Grigsby ended the conversation in Japanese with flawless annunciation.

He nodded at Ira and Sofia and sat in a tuft leather chair the color of chestnut. A grandfather clock began tolling nine bells. "Well, I'm famished."

"Shall I put in an order to the kitchen?" Sofia asked.

"No. Yacht Clubs seldom cook anything edible, only Country Clubs and Golf Clubs have proper chefs. Regardless, we're eating Sushi, I know a place in New Canaan. Let's go."

CHAPTER TWENTY-SIX

Sushi Lunatic

The Sushi restaurant smelled like seared fish and ginger. The hostess bowed and led them to their private paper walled room. Grigsby kicked off his Belgian loafers and hopped into the cube like a child in a ball pit. Ira looked around nervously, he hated raw fish but was willing to indulge given their victory.

Grigsby demanded their finest Sake and dinner to be Omakase. "Menus are for the ill-informed sheeple," he said. The hostess disappeared behind the paper doors. Minutes later they reopened, and Ira saw the frame of a wheelchair approach. It was Ryuki flanked by Bunny and Becky Pemberton.

Climbing from the chair, Grigsby ran over and hugged his butler. They spoke in Japanese and then sat. Sofia poured sake for the table, and Grigsby stood again to make a toast.

"We feast tonight not out of gluttony, spite, or even victory...no, tonight we celebrate life. Every morning I'm up before dawn. It's a ritual to watch the sun warm the room where ever I am. There's a component to this ritual where I acknowledge the people in my life who are alive and thriving. Everyone in this room I consider family and I love you all." Grigsby raised the ceramic cup with pooling eyes. Cheers erupted for Ryuki.

The first round of sushi rolls were ready. A hyperactive waiter flung open the door singing a Japanese pop song Grigsby knew from his time in Tokyo. In the midst of his dance, the waiter tripped, and the plates of sashimi began to fall. Then something miraculous happened. The waiter dropped to the ground like a soldier hitting the deck and caught each plate perfectly. The Pemberton's applauded. The waiter blushed and disappeared.

"What's the deal with that guy?" Sofia asked.

Grigsby's phone interrupted the conversation. It was the CEO of America's largest broadcasting corporation.

"Skip? Sorry about what happened tonight."

"Are you kidding me? It was fantastic, the carnage was a magnificent spectacle! Look, I don't have a lot of time, I wanted to offer you this before any of the other networks do." Skip continued to pitch Grigsby the idea of having *Very Ferry* inside a warehouse to satisfy all the safety components. Grigsby cut him off and agreed. "Terrific, I'll send over the paperwork now."

Grigsby hung up. Everyone at the table stared, waiting for him to say something. "Like my dear Ryuki, *Very Ferry* may never die!" The table celebrated. When the commotion settled down the waiter returned with a second platter and more sake.

Ira leaned over to Grigsby, "Who will be the new host?"

Grigsby held three rolls between the chopsticks and ate them at once, giving him the face of a sumo wrestler. He pointed to the waiter. "That lunatic." Ira smiled and knew it was the right choice.

The night continued on and Ryuki, now very drunk, declared his love for everyone in slurred Japanese. Grigsby explained that he forgets English when he's inebriated. Grigsby translated for the table. As the night wound down, a local baker opened the paper door. Grigsby had special ordered a gaggle of Baked Alaskas. Grigsby, now wearing a midnight blue sushi chef hat distributed the desserts while chanting: "*Very Ferry* may never die! *Very Ferry* may never die!"

San Francisco, California
Yosemite Valley, California
September 2, 2017 - September 27, 2017

Grigsby will be back soon.

Afterward

Grigsby Ives Pemberton is a force of nature and doesn't deserve to be constrained to a singular storyline. That's why I'm writing several more Grigsby stories. I've included a short story in this book about the early years of Grigsby's life. They're appropriately named, *Grigsby: The Origin Stories*. You can find them all on my website, for free. robertmaisano.com.

You can receive updates on this series and my forthcoming books by joining my community. Sign up on that page, and I'll send you a free book on why we all need fiction. Also, if you have story ideas let me know, happy to give you credit.

Thank you for reading. In a world of endless content, deciding to read my writings is the ultimate compliment, which I do not take lightly. I will always strive to provide great stories.

Introducing the Grigsby Origin Stories

After the launch of the first Grigsby novella, *Finding Bunny*, readers asked about his background, or stated "Grigsby would do something like that." I was happy to see the character take on a life of his own.

Grigsby is one of the most enjoyable characters to write about. Which is why I felt the need to color in his past. Imagining Grigsby as a young man getting into trouble in prep school seemed to be an appropriate place to start. Which is why I included that story in the second novella, *Picaroon Coast*. For this book, I wanted to move further into Grigsby's future. I felt that seeing him in an internship would be perfect.

The story you're about to read is the second origin story. It's about Grigsby working as an intern at a trading firm on Wall Street. Grigsby has a master understanding of the markets and how to out-leverage his peers and competitors. Since he's young he does not have his trading license, so he's befriended a man who trades off of Grigsby's advice. In the story, *The Wrath of the Intern*, we find Grigsby might have bitten off more than he could chew. Grigsby has to find a way to correct this massive position he's taken to save his friend's livelihood. Read on and see Grigsby battle the unpredictable forces of Wall Street in the 1980s.

The Wrath of the Intern

A Grigsby Origin Story

Glanton Leblanc Capital
45 Wall Street
Manhattan, New York

A trading floor on Wall Street is simple chaos. It may look like a room full of men shouting, but instead it's calculated amphetamine-fueled banter all aimed at one goal: money. If cash is king, Wall Street is the kingmaker. If you're decent at your, good for you here's a mortgage and a two bedroom house by the train tracks. If you're great, you earn a house far from the city, cloistered in neighborhoods with high hedges. It comes with a neurotic house wife who makes scenes at school board meetings. The rest of the money funds an apartment in the Bowery where the mistress lives. Grigsby wanted neither of these futures. He was interning so he could build an empire of his own.

Grigsby jogged down Water Street holding a file box filled with warm bagels. He had to feed the hungry traders before the opening bell. Grigsby j-walked like a pro. After dodging a city bus, he hailed a taxi so it would stop oncoming traffic. The taxi driver threw a can of Tab at him but Grigsby dodged that too.

He was sweating like a fat lady flying middle seat in coach. It's summertime in Manhattan. Street vendors doled out bagels and blue coffee cups to shifty eyed men in broad lapel suits. They all had dark thinning hair, no one knew if it was sweat or gel that kept it held back. The women in line were more foul-mouthed than the men.

Grigsby passed by the health club where all the bankers went before work. Most of them had memberships so they could use the steam rooms to flush out their hangovers.

Turning right on to Pine Street, Grigsby noticed one of the bagels at the top of the pile began to unfold from the cellophane wrapper. It sat inches from his face; the warm smell of poppy seeds, onion, and garlic trailed out—an everything bagel, Grigsby's favorite. "Screw it." Grigsby said as he bit into it while still holding the box. He pushed his neck forward like a sparrow eating from bird-feeder.

Nervous secretaries and arrogant bankers tilted their heads at Grigsby as he entered the offices of Glanton LeBlanc Capital, the world's most prestigious trading firm. They'd seen strange interns before but no one like Grigsby. Not only was he wearing egregiously expensive suits, impossible to afford on an intern's salary. But his knowledge of the markets shocked his colleagues and allowed him to throttle ahead of the other interns.

"He's like a mini-Buffet with better hair," one trader mocked as they saw Grigsby enter with box of bagels.

Traders, who were all nursing circadian hangovers, smiled when they smelled the fresh bagels. Leaning from their chairs, they seized the bagels from Grigsby in swift movements, like gypsies in a crowd. Some men grabbed five bagels at a time one hand and tossed them over green and black computer screens. Cigarettes, coffee, and bagels is the smell of Wall Street's fuel.

A man stepped out of a crammed office and pulled a cigarette from his mouth. "Pemberton!"

Grigsby went pale, it was Jackson, his boss.

"Get your ass in here."

The traders snickered and snatched the rest of the bagels from Grigsby as he hustled into the office. He shut the door, muffling the sounds of phones and shouts. The office smelled of old Chinese food and cigarettes. A horrible bouquet of scents, like the entire city of Hoboken had been stuffed into this tiny room.

Jackson was watching the printer buzz and clunk as it coughed out a leaf of paper. He tore it off and tossed it at Grigsby. "You mind explaining what the hell this trade is?"

Grigsby examined the slip. Mark, one of the traders, bought an $800,000 position yesterday before the market's close. Grigsby was the one who advised Mark to make the buy. Even though Grigsby was an intern, his knowledge of the markets are exceptional, but he doesn't have a license to trade stocks yet.

"What the hell is this mining company in...Go-ass?"

"Goiás, it's a region of Brazil that is rich with mineral veins—"

"Is this a long-term play?"

"No sir, we're unloading this puppy after the opening bell,"

Jackson stared at Grigsby with disdain. He was jealous of the boy's fortune, incredible mind, and hair. "You can't do this without my authorization Pemberton."

"We tried looking for you yesterday, I had to call an audible and convince Mark to make the trade." Grigsby said folding his arms, "Where were you anyway?"

Jackson looked away, biting his nails. "You better make this right." Jackson said deflecting the question.

"Not only will it be right, but we stand to make a sizable spread." Grigsby said.

"You better, or I'm firing Mark. He's got a baby on the way. Now get the hell out of my office."

Grigsby stood and left. He tried not to be jarred by the threat. Grigsby hustled to the box of bagels and frowned when he saw it was empty. "Savages." Grigsby muttered.

"Hey dude," said a low voice.

Grigsby turned and saw a hunk of muscles wrapped in pinstripes. "Morning Mark,"

"Jackson speak to you because of that trade?"

Grigsby nodded.

"Screw that guy. You understand the markets better them him." Mark took a seat beside his computer and stretched. "The numbers still look right to you? We're selling this fifteen minutes after the bell right?"

Grigsby didn't realize he was sweating profusely. Nervous about this new father losing his job if the trade goes south. Grigsby remembered what his father Ellison taught him, about keeping resolve. Grigsby reviewed the plan in his head again. The mining company was about to be granted rights to expand their mines to parcels of land that had never been excavated. This was a small blurb Grigsby read in a trade magazine. They bought low yesterday because this news hadn't hit the main papers. Right now, traders were reading about this news and readying to buy at open. Grigsby's plan was to sell at the first bump in the price boost. Grigsby looked at Mark and nodded.

They both turned and watched the clock count down to the market open.

When the trading bell sounds the lower tip of Manhattan glows green with greedy. Traders are shouting, signaling, tossing papers as they stare at the ticker symbols roll by. The stock exchange floor is as chaotic as a bar fight. But instead of fists and bottles it's bids and asks.

The first ten minutes of the market open are always terrifying. It's like standing on the back of a waking giant. Did it have a pleasant night sleep? Or did it have nightmares about mother-in-laws and ready to eat everyone in sight? No one ever knows.

Today, the giant seemed to be docile. Mark and Grigsby stood watching the ticker symbol flash across the wall. The stock was climbing as Grigsby expected. Mark ate a banana in two bites, waiting for the time to trade.

Grigsby checked his Omega watch, 5 minutes to go. "Mark, get your boys on the line. Let's get ready to dump this baby."

Mark hit speed dial and began to speak in a language few people outside a 212-area code know. Trader speak. It's a combination of incoherent fraternity banter, market data regurgitation, and ridiculous alliterations.

"Leone we got a live one here, flipping and flapping on the dock ready to swim, he goin' in your pool."

They proceeded to talk in fifteen second bursts. Then settled. "Okay at thirteen and an eighth, coming to you now. You're buying our next tee time, ciao." Mark hung up and stared at the screen. Grigsby held his breath and watched the trade go through and waited for the return to flash on screen.

Grigsby couldn't stare at the screen anymore and distracted himself with a Brazilian newspaper. He skimmed the headlines looking for another opportunity. There was nothing interesting, just the usual news. Farmers complaining about local taxes, soccer games being rained out, and a low supply of bikini wax.

"Holy hell…" Mark said. The return flashed on the screen: +25%. Grigsby exhaled a sigh of relief, they made a $200,000 profit. "Grigs you're an oracle."

"Print that out and deliver it to Jackson." Grigsby said.

"With pleasure," Mark high-fived Grigsby and pounded the keyboard. "Be back soon." Mark tore the leaf from the printer and ran to Jackson's office.

Grigsby smiled, reveling in relief. He opened another newspaper from Argentina and scanned the translated headlines. The news looked the same. Pestering local government, cancelled soccer games— Grigsby froze and compared the stories about the cancelled soccer games. Both reports cited heavy rainfall over the last week. Grigsby's eyes widened, he took the newspapers and hurried down the hall toward the Research Department.

The Research Department, nicknamed *The Morgue*, is a place never graced by sunlight. The people shuffle from the break room to re-heat last night's cod dinners and the coffee is changed once a week. It's hell for Grigsby to be in. It's a sad illustration of complacency in the most opportunistic country in the world.

Grigsby moved through the cubicle maze to find the person he needed. He poked his head around a cubicle and startled a pale man in a short sleeve white button-down shirt. He was clipping out a *Dilbert* comic strip from the newspaper.

"Barry, where's Sweaters?" Grigsby asked.

"She's out. Taking a Stay-cation." Barry answered.

Grigsby gagged, the thought of using your vacation time to stay at home physically disgusted him. "I need to get rainfall data for South America, can you do this for me?"

Barry rubbed the back of his neck, "Oh jeeze, my lunch break is coming up—"

Grigsby pulled a $100 bill from his jacket pocket, "Here, a year supply of street-meat. Pull that data now."

Barry pocketed the money and swiveled to his computer. Grigsby paced inside the cubicle as the man punched the keys. Twenty minutes later the printer clunked and buzzed and spat out the data Grigsby needed. He tore it off and reread. "So, over the past 10 years, there's been heavy rain, months before their so-called rainy season?"

Barry pushed his glasses atop his nose, "Yes, it looks like August has been consistent, the model here shows itself already repeating the cycle." He pointed to the most recent data, "The rain has already begun, it looks like it'll be another wet month for them."

"Terrific!" Grigsby patted Barry's back so hard it knocked the wind out of him. Grigsby sprinted down the hall back to the trading floor.

Mark was scarfing down Chinese food from a Styrofoam container while on the phone. Grigsby arrived in front of him out of breath. "Mark hang up. You need to hear me out."

"Can this wait? I'm trying to put a grand on the Mets."

"Mark, this is huge."

Mark rolled his eyes, "I'll call you back." He hung up. "What is it Grigsby?"

Grigsby flattened out the sheet of rainfall data and pulled the two newspapers. "There's going to be flooding in Brazil. Right where the mining company is."

Mark's eye brows raised and he scanned the data. Grigsby leaned over and snatched his eggroll. "Dammit Grigsby that was mine,"

"Focus Mark." Grigsby chomped away at the deep-fried burrito.

"Okay looks right, but so what? We sold out position who cares about them?"

"We need to short them, heavily, you should put all your money on this."

"Grigsby, that's over a million, I can't—"

"Look what you stand to gain." Grigsby handed a post-it note with precise arithmetic written fastidiously across it.

"Oh my..."

The phone rang and like with a Pavlovian response Mark leaned forward and picked it up on the first ring. It was a curt conversation. Mark only said, "Yes sir," several times and hung up.

"Mark what's wrong?" Grigsby asked.

Mark stared at his black and green computer screen. He became pale as the ceiling.

"Mark?" Grigsby asked again.

Mark spoked, but still faced the screen, "Jackson saw the trade, he didn't care about the profit."

"What? That's a better return than any of these monkeys could make in a week." Grigsby was serenaded in a chorus of New York profanities from the other traders who heard him. He ducked from the office supplies being thrown and waited for them to settle down and keep trading. Grigsby pulled a chair close to Mark. "How could Jackson not care?"

"He said I shouldn't be taking advice from an intern." Mark said burying his head in his palms.

"Jackson doesn't want to look like he's uninformed. Which, he damn well is, he's management, they all rise to the level of their incompetence."

"I know but he's the boss Grigsby."

"What if he didn't have to be?" Grigsby said, he grabbed a whiteboard and wrote across it: "Is Jackson An Asshole?" He showed it around the room. The traders smirked and gave thumbs up. "See? No one likes him, what if we can get everyone here to short the stock? The firm would stand to hit historic gains."

"No one will listen to you Grigsby, I'm the only one."

Grigsby shook his head, "It wouldn't be me doing selling, it'll be Chloe." Grigsby said pointing across the floor.

Chloe McNamara, senior at Florida State, couldn't tell the difference between a mortgage from a potato. Grigsby thought the sheer volume of bleach she uses had seeped into her brain cavity long ago. Since she was a *Florida Gal* she wore pencils skirts that ended miles from the knee, thus earning her the name, "the skintern." Nevertheless, she was the best sales person Wall Street had ever seen.

Chloe always wanted to be an actress but realized there's more money in memorizing a script on Wall Street. Wearing a low blouse and reciting market data can convince 90% of Wall Street to buy.

Grigsby came by her desk and noticed she was flicking bits of food into her Birkin bag. "Interesting diet", Grigsby thought. When Chloe saw Grigsby approach she stopped and composed herself.

"Grigsby how are you my dear?" Chloe said with the tone like they hadn't seen each other in years. Grigsby sat down beside her and began explaining the situation. He needed her to convince all the traders to short the Brazilian mining company's stock. He explained the key figures she needed to cite.

Chloe began rehearsing her sales pitch to Grigsby when he noticed her bag was moving. "Oh dear, Munchkin go back to sleep," Chloe said to the bag, but it kept moving. She reached in and pulled out an ash-amber Yorkie, complete with a stupid bow on the forehead. Grigsby's sunk his head into his palms.

"Chloe, the market's closing soon," Grigsby stated.

She continued rehearsing while holding her Yorkie in the fold of her arm. Grigsby listened and wondered how they had the same job.

"Whatcha think?" Chloe asked.

"Lovely, now go, I'll watch Munchkin," Grigsby said as he took the tiny dog in his arms. Chloe hustled away taking short strides so as not to trip in her Louboutins. Grigsby looked at Munchkin, it sniffed and licked his hands. "C'mon Munchkin, let's go say hello to Jackson."

Jackson was in his office trying to assess what would bankrupt him first: the second mortgage on his home in Greenwich, the mortgage on his home in Montauk, or his boat loan. Jackson got heartburn when he saw Grigsby approach with a tiny dog that had a stupid bow on its head.

"Chloe has a sales call and asked if you can watch Munchkin," Grigsby stated, plopping the dog on his desk amongst leafs of paper.

"What? Grigsby get the hell out of here."

"She asked only for you." Grigsby declared.

Jackson leaned back in his chair flattered. The thoughts of her blonde hair and Chanel No. 5 erased his concerns about the mountains of looming debt. He smiled. This is why men have affairs, it's not the lust, or vanity, it's to forget about the treacherous credit card statements and account balances that hold up their lives like a wet house of cards. Jackson agreed.

"Great, well here's the dog's favorite toy, have fun." Grigsby rushed out of the office.

The final hour of trading had begun.

New Yorkers have a distinct talent of communicating silently. It's a combination of synchronized eye movements and lip reading. This isn't taught in business school. It's something you learn when riding the subways. It's the best method to say smug insults to your friend about the guy across from you. This is also how most news is spread in the office, hushed tones. Effective for stealth but not when you need to spread the word fast.

Grigsby figured that's how Chloe would deliver the news. He checked his watch as he hustled to the trading desks. 50 minutes left. Grigsby worried that this wouldn't be enough time to convince the individual traders. To his surprise Chloe had found another way to spread the message.

She was standing atop one of the desks. Commanding all the traders to listen. Chloe delivered her rehearsed pitch with gusto. The traders smirked at first but after hearing the numbers started to get serious. They took notes in the margins of newspapers and on scraps of Telex.

Grigsby smiled as he watched Chloe climb off the desk and the traders all picked up their phones. Grigsby picked up a phone too and dialed the concierge number at his favorite hotel in Rio de Janeiro.

"Ritz Carlton Concierge, Guilherme speaking,"

"Gil, it's Grigsby I need a favor,"

"Ah Master Pemberton, of course. Shall I inform the chef of your arrival, he usually needs 24 hours to prepare for your visits."

"No, no, though Chef Luiz's Baked Alaska would hit the spot right now I need to get some information about the weather situation down there."

Guilherme sounded like he was frowning when he told Grigsby of the ceaseless rain.

"Excellent and what about the State of Goiás?"

"Hmm, I'll phone our sister hotel, stay on the line."

Grigsby waited five minutes, then ten. A half hour remained and the traders were screaming like petulant adolescents from a royal family. The stock price they were trying to short was still climbing, the opposite of what Grigsby wanted.

Mark watched the screen as he bit his thumbnail. "Grigsby...this ain't looking good."

Grigsby listened to nothingness through the receiver. "C'mon Guilherme, c'mon."

Some of the traders through up their hands and refused to short the stock. Traders are like Wildebeests, it only takes one to panic and create a dangerous stampede.

"Master Pemberton?" Guilherme said.

"Talk to me."

"I couldn't get a hold of our sister hotel in Goiás."

Time slowed, fear overwhelmed Grigsby. He realized that without convincing the reluctant traders it wouldn't work. He needed everyone to short the stock. Guilherme was speaking again but Grigsby didn't hear. "What?"

"I'm saying that they're phone lines are down most likely because of flooding. I called the nearby hospital because they have generators and the nurse confirmed there's heavy flooding."

"Thank you Guilherme," Grigsby hung up and climbed on Marks desk, shouting for everyone's attention.

The traders rolled their eyes, "Mr. Peanut wants to talk to us," said one of the traders. Grigsby ignored their disdain and informed them of the flooding, saying it's no longer a prediction but real. No one spoke. Then the ten minute buzzer rang— all of a sudden the reluctant traders picked up their phones and shorted the stock.

Grigsby sat down and exhaled several times, Mark patted his back. "You're an animal Grigsby, let's hope this works."

Grigsby Ives Pemberton never made it in the *Wall Street Journal* during his internship. Though the men and women he helped did. As the flooding increased the stock continued to plummet and they sold right as it bottomed out. Grigsby gave all the credit to Mark. The company's Board fired Jackson and made Mark the boss.

A few months later Grigsby received a check from Mark. It was large enough to make a communist weep. Grigsby chuckled and routed the lump sum to Guilherme with explicit instruction that it go to relieve the suffering area in Goiás. Grigsby, channeling grace, wrote a small note which read: "Keep this anonymous. Depois da tempestade vem a bonança."

About the Author

Robert Maisano is a writer, speaker, and award-winning marketer. He's written for *Business Insider* and *Thought Catalog*. Robert launched the Grigsby series as a daily serial, for free, on robertmaisano.com. He lives in San Francisco.

A Note On The Type

The typeface used throughout the novella is a serif design from the 1750s created by John Baskerville in Birmingham, England which was then cut into metal by John Handy (appropriate name).

The style is classified as a transitional typeface. Earlier designs of the typeface increased the contrast between thick and thin strokes, which make the serifs a bit more tapered and sharper. Baskerville is one of the many popular typefaces used in book design.

A non-scientific study conducted in 2012 asserted that readers of the Baskerville typeface increased the likelihood of the reader agreeing with the prose by 1.5% when compared to other fonts such as Georgia, Helvetica, Trebuchet, and the ever so silly Comic Sans.

Now if you ever meet a designer or a calligrapher you have a nice tidbit of information that'll make you appear wiser in front of them.

Biplane Media

BOOKS | FILM | RADIO
SF • NYC

At Biplane Media, we support creatives who make perennially stunning content. We're dedicated to capturing adventure in everyday life and finding the wonder that hides around the world.

The gatekeepers are gone. As access to digital mediums proliferates throughout the world, it's easier for us to distribute our art to you. We don't have to rely on getting picked by a top publishing house or major studio. We can show our art as easily as we can make it now.

What does this all mean?

Since we're independent and at the forefront of content distribution, we promise to price our work accordingly. The goal is to make it as accessible as possible. The entire *Grigsby Series* is available online for free. If you enjoy what we make the highest compliment is to share it with friends. Spreading the word and growing this community will allow us to venture into more exciting projects.

If you're a creator and have something you'd like to share, we'd be happy to chat. Drop by our site: www.biplane.media to get in touch. Everyone has a story in them, we're here to help tell it.

Continue Reading

All of the stories from the *Grigsby Series* can be found at robertmaisano.com.

Keep In Touch

Search my name into your favorite social network and say hello.

Very Ferry